My season with Penguins
An Antarctic Journal

sophie Webb

Houghton Mifflin Company
Boston

To my parents, Nancy and Bill Webb, and to the Antarctic with the hope that it remains unexploited and unclaimed by any country and a haven for wildlife in perpetuity.

The text of this book is set in Stone Serif.
The illustrations are watercolor, gouache, and graphite.

Library of Congress Cataloging-in-Publication Data
Webb, Sophie.
My season with penguins : an Antarctic journal / Sophie Webb.
p.   cm.
Summary: Describes the author's two-month stay in Antarctica to study and draw penguins.
RNF ISBN 0-395-92291-7   PAP ISBN 0-618-43234-5
1. Adélie Penguin — Antarctica — Juvenile literature. [1. Adélie Penguin. 2. Penguins. 3. Antarctica.] I. Title.
QL696.S473   W42   2000
598.47 — dc21
99-054781

Design by Lynne Yeamans

Printed in Singapore
TWP 10 9 8 7 6 5 4

Acknowledgments

There are innumerable people who contributed to the making of this book, and I regret anyone that I may leave out. First I must thank David Ainley — without his invitation to work on his project, this book would not have been possible. I thank all whom I shared the penguins with during three seasons at Cape Royds: Connie Adams, David Ainley, Grant Ballard, Mike Beigel, Ian Gaffney, Denise Hardesty, Sacha Heath, Nat Polish, Chris Ribic, Sue Townsend, and Stephani Zador. I also thank Kerry Barton, Peter Wilson, and B.J. Karl, all from Land Care Research New Zealand, our New Zealander colleagues in the Adélie project; and the folks from the New Zealand Heritage Trust: David, Peter, Lawrence, Sara, and Sheridan. I thank everyone at McMurdo for support, in particular, at McMurdo Operations, Mary, Shelly, Annie, Lesia, and Clay; at the BFC (Berg Field Center), Mimi and Cathy; at Helo Operations, Robin and all her staff. I am also grateful to H. T. Harvey and Associates and PRBO (Point Reyes Bird Observatory) for their support. The National Science Foundation funded Dr. David Ainley's portion of the Adélie project. Any mistakes in information are solely my responsibility. I also thank Ann Rider, my editor, for many helpful comments on the text. And last I must thank Steve Howell for editorial comments, encouragement, and patience.

I've traveled in many countries painting, drawing, and studying birds. For years I dreamed of going to Antarctica to see penguins. Never did I think this would become a reality, but in 1996 I was invited by David Ainley to join his project studying Adélie Penguins in the Antarctic. It was an opportunity to live with penguins for two months during the Antarctic summer. I jumped at the chance.

An Adélie Penguin,
PYGOSCELIS ADELIAE

01 December

This is the beginning of my long journey south, and halfway around the globe. I start by taking a bus from my home to the airport in San Francisco, where I meet the rest of the U.S. contingent of our research group: David, Grant, Ian, Sacha, and Sue. We board the plane and make the eleven-hour flight to New Zealand, the last stop in civilization before the Antarctic.

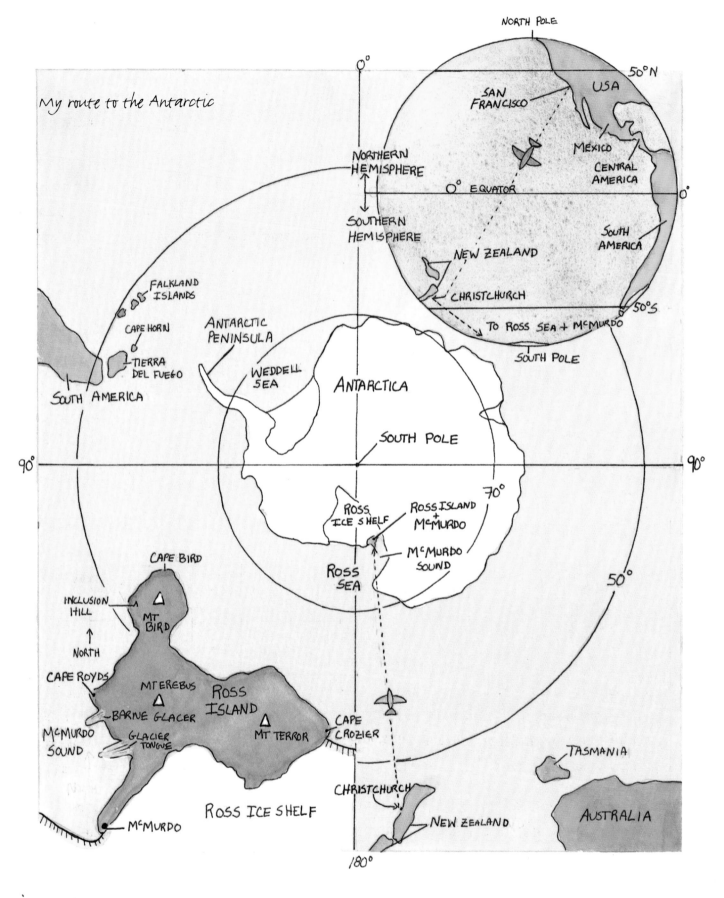

My route to the Antarctic

NORTH POLE

50°N

USA

SAN FRANCISCO

MEXICO

CENTRAL AMERICA

NORTHERN HEMISPHERE

0° EQUATOR

SOUTHERN HEMISPHERE

NEW ZEALAND

SOUTH AMERICA

CHRISTCHURCH

50°S

TO ROSS SEA + McMURDO

SOUTH POLE

FALKLAND ISLANDS

CAPE HORN

TIERRA DEL FUEGO

SOUTH AMERICA

ANTARCTIC PENINSULA

WEDDELL SEA

ANTARCTICA

SOUTH POLE

ROSS ICE SHELF

ROSS ISLAND + McMURDO

McMURDO SOUND

ROSS SEA

70°

90°

90°

50°

CAPE BIRD

INCLUSION HILL

MT BIRD

NORTH

CAPE ROYDS

MT EREBUS

ROSS ISLAND

BARNE GLACIER

GLACIER TONGUE

McMURDO SOUND

MT TERROR

CAPE CROZIER

TASMANIA

AUSTRALIA

CHRISTCHURCH

NEW ZEALAND

ROSS ICE SHELF

McMURDO

180°

03 December

It's 07:30 (we use a twenty-four-hour clock) and there's land below, the North Island of New Zealand. We land in Auckland, where it is cloudy and warm — summer weather. We're in the Southern Hemisphere now, where the seasons are reversed from back home in California.

We get our baggage: six large boxes filled with computers and other scientific equipment and several bags with our personal gear. We are a spectacle in the airport, where we sit and wait for our flight to Christchurch on the South Island of New Zealand. Finally, after a half-hour delay, we're on our way.

Sue follows me through customs with our huge boxes of equipment.

Upon our arrival in Christchurch we are met at the airport by the National Science Foundation (NSF)/Antarctic Support Associates (ASA) representative. She tells us that we must go directly to the Clothing Distribution Center to try on all our "Extreme Cold Weather" clothing because tomorrow morning we are scheduled to fly to McMurdo, one of the United States Antarctic Program's bases.

The Clothing Distribution Center is a blocky building, part of a complex of offices and a museum devoted to Antarctic research and exploration. Basically, it's a warehouse *full* of clothing and stored equipment, and an office. When I walk in I am confronted with a wall covered with all the possible

Dressing for the Antarctic

clothing types: red jackets for NSF grantees and employees, brown ones for ASA staff, and a myriad of different gloves, mittens, hats, long underwear, and boots. On each side of the entrance there is a changing room, one for men, one for women. Sacha, Sue, and I enter the latter and each find two large orange bags filled with clothing to try on. The fluorescent lights whine and flicker as we fling long underwear, down jackets, and wind pants about the room. It's utter chaos. Half-dressed women run back and forth exchanging items for ones in different sizes. Sweat begins to run down my arms, my back. It's summer in New Zealand and these clothes we're trying on are designed for the Antarctic cold. At McMurdo in August, the Antarctic winter, the temperature averages –72°F (–22°C); however, in January, the summer, the temperature averages 30°F (–1°C). Finally I find clothing that fits reasonably well. Next I attempt to stuff books, paints, paper, and cameras into the two orange bags provided. For me this is a struggle. The last items I pick up are my dog tags. These are two metal tags with my name and project number on them. We are supposed to wear these whenever we fly, in case we crash. Our bodies would then be readily identified. A gruesome thought.

04 December

Our flight to McMurdo, Antarctica, is delayed for a day due to poor weather.

05 December

We get to the Clothing Distribution Center by 06:00 and change into our warm clothing, put on our dog tags, check in, have breakfast, and wait. Finally, we're loaded onto a bus. We make our way to the runway, where the New Zealand Royal Air Force plane awaits us. It's a military cargo carrier, low-slung and potbellied with four turbo engines, two per side. We're ushered from the bus to one side of the pavement to wait while the plane is being loaded.

As we wait to board, a large pallet—covered with boxes of fresh produce and the orange bags filled with personal gear—is slowly pulled up the ramp at the tail of the plane.

After a half-hour we are allowed to board the plane. The "seats" made of red webbing are really not much more than benches flanking each side of the plane. I sit at the end of a bench. Next to me there is a huge stack of boxes containing lettuce and eggs strapped to the floor. The engines finally start, and the plane begins shimmying down the runway. There are only a few sparsely placed portholes on each side, so I feel, rather than watch, the takeoff. After fifteen minutes the engines stop their straining and relax. I look around and everyone I see is either reading or napping. Conversation is impossible due to the engine noise, and everyone is wearing earplugs.

Napping on the plane

Nine hours later we land on a runway on the sea ice next to Ross Island in the Ross Sea. It's a beautiful sunny day, 30°F (–1°C), with a bit of wind, the Royal Society Mountains majestic in the distance. We climb into an enormous bus called Ivan the Terra-Bus, and drive slowly across the sea ice, past Scott Base (New Zealand), and finally to McMurdo. It's a small, desolate town of prefabricated, corrugated sheet metal buildings, snowy and dirty. In the peak of the summer season it can house more than one thousand personnel. McMurdo is one of several U.S. (and numerous international) bases in the Antarctic devoted to scientific research and exploration. An international treaty designates the Antarctic as a continent used only for peaceful purposes — that is, mostly scientific research. Treaties signed in 1978, 1984, and the early 1990s dictate that the Antarctic's land and ocean environments will not be disturbed by humankind's activities. Every scientist that works in the U.S. Antarctic program must show that his or her research will have little or no detrimental impact on the environment. There are no territorial borders and no part of the Antarctic is owned by a country.

Now it's about 18:00 (6 P.M.); we have dinner and go to a short orientation meeting. Then we gather our gear and return to our dormitory rooms to sleep. Tomorrow will be a long day.

06 December

 Up early after a restless sleep. It will take a while for me to get used to the twenty-four-hour daylight.

We eat breakfast, then go to a waste management meeting. Just about everything in McMurdo gets recycled or reused because it's so difficult to get resupplied and to dispose of trash. Later we meet with the National Science Foundation support staff, followed by another meeting with McMurdo Operations, the center of radio communications. The people working here will be our link to McMurdo from our field camps. We will report to them daily by radio to let them know that all is well and to inform them when we need to send samples back to the lab or need a resupply of food or other camp goods, have an emergency—or simply want to chat.

We spend the rest of the day sorting and testing our scientific equipment in the Crary Laboratory.

07 December

 We go to survival school to learn about some of the hazards and pleasures of camping and working in the Antarctic. A storm of high winds and blowing snow can appear suddenly and cause a complete whiteout. This means one can't see more than a few feet. It's easy to get disoriented and cold in such conditions. If not prepared with some basic survival skills people can, and do,

The view from the Crary Laboratory showing part of McMurdo Station and the fast ice covering McMurdo Sound to the Royal Society Mountains

die of hypothermia. At night we camp out on the sea ice in tents and snow caves that we built. We are fortunate that it is a relatively warm, sunny, and still evening. I have trouble sleeping again because of the bright light, and because I'm excited to be camping in the Antarctic.

08 December

Today Sue and I pick out our camp equipment and food for the season. The supply room for dried and canned goods is set up as a small, well-organized supermarket, and there is almost as much choice. We certainly are not going to starve. Fortunately, there also seems to be an endless supply of chocolate, probably one of the most important items in any Antarctic diet. Chocolate combined with nuts makes a quick high-energy snack—we burn up a lot of calories in the cold. It takes us several hours to pick out our food for two months, box it, and weigh it. Everything must be weighed, because helicopters don't fly well if overloaded. We have sixteen hundred pounds of scientific gear and food, not including ourselves.

12 December

Penguins walking across the remaining fast ice to McMurdo sound; the Trans-Antarctic Range in the distance

The weather has been stormy, so we have been stuck at McMurdo for several days. Ian flew out earlier this morning. He'll be working with our New Zealander colleagues at Cape Bird. Now it's 11:00 and the rest of us — Sacha, David, Grant, Sue, and I — are out on the helicopter pad with all our gear, ready to fly to Cape Royds. The others are going to help Sue and me for a day or two. Soon the five of us and all the equipment are loaded into the helicopter and we are up in the air skimming over the sea ice heading north. We pass Big Razor Back and a rookery of several hundred Weddell seals, Tent and Inaccessible Islands, and the Barne Glacier that spills off Mount Erebus. The view is spectacular and my heart is in my throat in anticipation of seeing the penguins.

After a half-hour we arrive at Cape Royds. It's windy but beautiful. In one direction Mount Erebus looms over us; in another we can look down a slight incline past Shackleton's hut to the Adélie Penguin colony on cliffs overlooking McMurdo Sound. The fast ice (a solid sheet of frozen ocean held fast to the land) here ends abruptly with a white edge against dark blue water. The sun comes out and everything sparkles.

Our living quarters have been completely set up by carpenters from McMurdo. The Polar Haven is an eight-by-twelve-foot, semipermanent tent with a plywood floor, somewhat insulated cloth walls, a propane heater, two windows, and a door with a splendid view across McMurdo Sound. It couldn't be more ideal. We will cook, eat, organize data, and relax here. Solar panels will charge all our batteries and run our computers.

Outside is our toilet with a view of the mountains. It is an old ammunition box with a plastic bag and a toilet seat of plywood and Styrofoam. We pee separately into a barrel. Because of the cold and dryness and lack of bacteria, nothing decays here; therefore, everything is packaged up and taken back to either McMurdo or the United States for disposal.

Our camp with the Polar Haven and our sleeping tents (Sue's is purple and mine is yellow). Grant, David, and Sacha will share our sleeping tents or sleep in the Polar Haven for the next few days.

I walk down to the colony. Adélie Penguins are true dwellers of the Antarctic; only the large Emperor Penguin breeds as far south. Here at Cape Royds, at latitude 77°33' south, we are at the most southerly Adélie Penguin colony in the world. It's a small colony, only 3,600 pairs, while the other colonies being studied in the project range from 30,000 to 150,000 pairs. The penguin colony is a pale ocher patch surrounded by dark gray rocks speckled with black and white lumps. As I walk closer the lumps begin to take shape — the Adélies. They are comical, and it's hard not to think of them as little people with their

Ecstatic display

Positioning an egg

waddling gait, upright posture, rotund bellies, and odd expressive eyes. Troops of them head out across the fast ice to the sea. They pause and hop over a crack, then run and skid onto their bellies using their tails as rudders, their feet pushing them forward, as they toboggan across the ice.

In the colony I see a few males display. Their flippers are held out to each side and flap, their bills pointed skyward, eyes rolling backward exaggerating their whites, and a weird *eh-eh-eh-eh* noise erupting from their chests. This is the "ecstatic display," used to attract the opposite sex.

Greeting

Tobogganing

About a month ago, in the beginning of November, the male Adélies returned to the colony to choose a nest site. Usually this is the same site they occupied in the previous year, if they bred. Several days later the females arrived and chose a mate, frequently the same male as the one they bred with the year before. The Adélies have a series of ritualistic displays that help to form the pair bond (the ecstatic display being one of them). It may take several days for the pair bond to form and copulation to take place. A week to ten days later the female will lay the first egg, the second egg a day or two later. Then the female will leave the nest to feed for up to two weeks. The male stays behind to incubate the eggs. This means that the male Adélie, from the time he first arrives, will fast for four to five weeks. When the female Adélie returns, she will incubate the eggs for about ten days while the male is out feeding; thereafter they trade places more frequently until time spent away from the nest decreases to a day or less. This is about the time the eggs hatch. Incubation takes about five weeks.

Most of the birds are lying horizontally, still incubating, when we arrive, but a few eggs have already hatched. I can hear the soft peeps of the new chicks among the adults' greeting brays.

An incubating bird (lying horizontally). The eggs are placed on top of the feet and tucked up into a warm brood pouch, a loose pocket of warm, vascularized (filled with veins) skin.

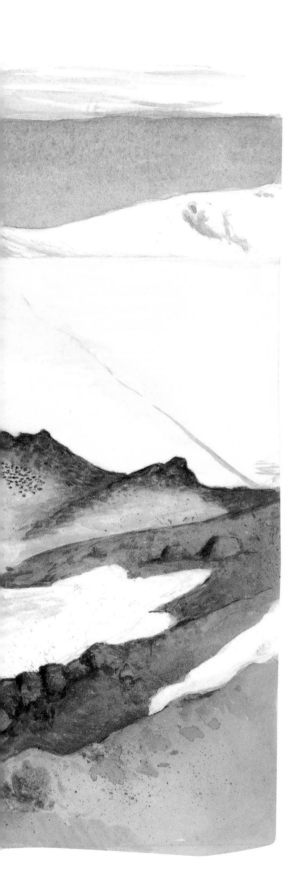

In the evening, back at camp, the sky is gray and spitting snow. I forgot how much I hate going outside to pee when it's cold and windy.

The view from our camp down to the penguin colony. Shackleton's hut is on the left, Mount Discovery in the distance.

14 December

Grant, David, Sacha, Sue, and I spend the day hauling batteries, boxes, and fencing down the hill from camp into the colony.

The penguin colony is divided into smaller subcolonies, which range in size from as few as five nests to as many as several hundred. One of these subcolonies is our experimental plot. It has about 180 nests. We create a corral with orange plastic fencing around the subcolony, leaving only one exit,

A banded penguin crosses the weigh bridge.

where an electronic "weigh bridge" is placed. Whenever the penguins go in or out of the colony, they will be weighed. (Adult Adélies weigh about three to four kilos, or six and a half to nine pounds.) Subtracting a penguin's "in" weight from its "out" weight will tell us how much food it fed to its chicks. This way we don't have to handle the birds to weigh them. On the bridge there is an electronic hoop. We will mark seventy penguins with flipper bands and PIT tags (a small cylinder that reads like a bar code). The electronic hoop will read the PIT tags. In this way we will keep track of seventy individuals for the season. It takes the Adélies a couple days to become used to their new exit.

This season is only the first of a six-year study. In order to understand the natural fluctuations in any ecosystem, one needs years of data. One year can be drastically different from another, and it is only over time that the entire picture can become clear. Each year for two months there will be a small group of researchers from the USA and New Zealand who take data at the three Adélie Penguin colonies on Ross Island. Some of the questions we are trying to answer are

How do the colonies on Ross Island relate to one another? Why are some of the colonies very large and some small?

Is there much movement of birds between colonies?

Is there overlap in their feeding areas?

How do weather and ice conditions affect each of the colonies?

Why do Adélie populations seem to be increasing this far south of the Antarctic and decreasing to the north?

Could this increase be due to a change in ice conditions, and if so, perhaps a response to global warming?

By understanding these dynamics in a relatively simple ecosystem (if anything in the natural world can be called simple) and an environment that has had relatively little impact from man, we may be able to apply what we learn to other populations of sea birds in the Antarctic and to other parts of the world where there is more impact from fisheries, tourism, and oil spills.

Dinner seems to take forever as we cook for five on the Coleman stove. We make a stir-fry of frozen vegetables and shrimp with a spicy peanut sauce. It's fairly easy to keep food frozen in the Antarctic. Fortunately, we cook a lot of food so there will be leftovers for tomorrow.

Later in the evening, about 21:00 (9:00 P.M.), I walk down to the colony to paint, but I forget to add a little alcohol to my painting water to prevent it from freezing. My paints turn to slush on the paper.

16 December

Grant, David, and Sacha have left for their respective camps of Cape Crozier and Cape Bird, leaving Sue and me here to continue the fieldwork at Cape Royds.

After our daily chores, we spend the rest of the day banding penguins. In order to band a penguin we must first catch it. Adélie Penguins have very little fear on land. They evolved in an isolated environment in which adults have had virtually no terrestrial predators. Their lack of fear means that we can

Four penguin bands taped together, a single band showing the unique number, pliers for closing the metal band, and a field notebook for notes and data that will be entered into our computer later

approach them easily. When incubating they stay tight on their nest, lying horizontally, the eggs on their feet and tucked up into a brood pouch. Trying to disturb the colony as little as possible, Sue bends over, grabs an incubating penguin, and maneuvers the bird's body and flippers under her arm so its head peeks out behind, much like a large football. She places my wool hat over the eggs to keep them warm. Then she holds the bird while I put on the metal flipper band and attach a PIT tag. Penguins are hard and muscular, designed to move swiftly through cold water, so we often come away with a few good pecks and bruises (who can blame them?). After banding, Sue places the penguin gently on the ground next to its nest and releases it. It fusses a bit, then sits back on its nest.

The flipper bands allow us to follow individual penguins from year to year. Penguins are very faithful about returning to a colony where they have bred in previous years, and they can live for at least fourteen years. If the marked adults do not return the following year, we can assume that they have died.

Sue catches a penguin at a nest.

Emperor Penguin Standing

Walking

Tobogganing

Being investigated by an Adélie

Trumpeting

Neck extended looking about

Today two tall Emperor Penguins are out on the fast ice, dwarfing the Adélies. They have blackish feet that they stare at periodically. One Emperor lifts its head and lets out a trumpet. They breed on an ice tongue off Beaufort Island, which is about thirty miles (fifty kilometers) to the north of Cape Royds.

The constant daylight is disorienting and makes it easy to forget time is passing. There are none of the daily markers that rule our lives. Before I know it, it is 01:00 (1 A.M.).

A day-old chick

As the chicks get fatter, only their heads fit in the brood pouch. Their large, fluffy butts look like enormous fuzzy slippers.

18 December

I spend some time walking around the colony. About half the eggs have hatched. There are many silvery gray chicks with large dark heads, blackish bills with whitish tips, and thin peeping voices. They have enormous feet and tiny wings. Newly hatched chicks are completely dependent on the adult for warmth, which the adult's brood pouch provides.

Nests are placed just pecking distance apart.

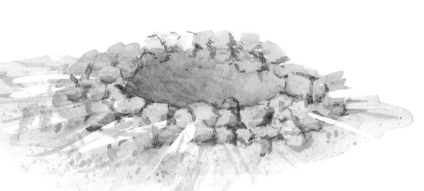

Adélie digging a nest scrape with its foot

An empty penguin nest

The Adélie nest is a shallow scrape (a depression dug in the ground by a penguin). The rim is formed by small rocks that the birds have collected. These rocks are much prized. A very large nest of rocks is often an indicator of a bird's stature — signifying, for example, a bird's level of fitness or its success as a parent. I see a bird sneak up behind another that is sleeping, stretch out its neck, and gently steal a stone from the edge of the nest. The almost sly expression on its face turns to guilt as its theft is discovered. It hurries back to its nest with its prize.

Carrying a rock

stealing a rock from an incubating bird

shackleton's hut being inspected by the penguins; Mount Erebus, a still-active volcano, smoking in the background

Walking back up from the colony I see a group of curious Adélies inspecting the outside of Shackleton's hut. They poke and stare at the piles of wooden crates and rusty wheels. These are supplies left over from Sir Ernest Shackleton's expedition in 1908–9. He and the fourteen men on his team built the hut and wintered at Cape Royds before making an attempt to be the first to reach the South Pole. Shackleton and his team were unsuccessful in their try for the Pole, but they did gather a large amount of scientific information during their stay. Their isolation must have been incredible. Unlike present-day scientists and explorers, they had no radios, no mid-winter drops of mail and supplies from planes; they had no contact with the outside world for most of a year.

The hut remains intact, still filled with many of the original canned foods, reindeer hide sleeping bags, and other supplies that Shackleton left behind for use by future explorers stranded at Cape Royds. Currently the hut is maintained as a historic site, a small museum of early exploration. The penguins find it fascinating.

20 December

Today we attach radio transmitters to fifteen penguins. Each transmitter is tuned to a unique frequency. This will allow us to track individual penguins when they go out to sea to feed. Then we can find out if there is any overlap of feeding areas between the colonies. The adult penguins with chicks can be extremely defensive, which makes them difficult to catch without getting painful bruises. Once Sue catches a penguin, she holds it as still as possible with its rear facing me. Using waterproof tape I quickly attach the transmitter to the feathers on the lower back of the penguin and the bird is returned to its nest. The transmitters should stay on for about three weeks and then we will remove them.

A porpoising penguin with a radio transmitter

A penguin with a radio transmitter and its ten-day-old chick

The wind dies in the evening. The ocean is a cold blue-gray, littered with pack ice (broken fast ice, packed tightly together, that is moved around on the ocean surface by winds and currents). The penguins squawk out on the fast ice as they wend their way out to the water. They erupt from the water like rockets and land on the ice floes (single pieces of pack ice) upright or on their bellies, bouncing and sliding across the ice.

The view from our telemetry hill, north to Mount Bird and Inclusion Hill

Inclusion Hill and Sacha

21 December

Up early in the morning to check the radio telemetry receiver. The receiver is tuned to record the fifteen different frequencies of the radio transmitters. From the receiver we learn which penguins are in the colony and by their absence we learn the duration of their foraging trips. Here at Cape Royds the Adélies generally do not go very far, and their trips are usually no more than twelve to eighteen hours. At Cape Crozier and other colonies the birds can be out for two days or more. Back at camp I talk with the other camps to find out which of their birds are out foraging: they are the ones I need to listen for. Then I walk to the top of our telemetry hill, where I stand, antenna in hand, headphones on, and our portable receiver over my shoulder. There I listen for the Cape Royds' penguins not recorded in the colony this morning and try to hear any of the Cape Bird penguins that Sacha has heard. She's twenty miles away, on Mount Bird's Inclusion Hill, and talks to me over a hand-held voice radio. We'll listen for our birds three times a day for the next three weeks. Today it's beautiful up here on the

Listening for birds with radio transmitters

hill, not too cold. It can be bitter and windy. I can see a pod of killer whales swimming in McMurdo Sound, their long fins jutting out of the water among the pack ice.

Killer whales eat fish and Weddell seals.

By now almost all of the eggs have hatched. Some parents have two equal-sized chicks, while others have chicks that are markedly different in size. In years when there is a lot of food available, the Adélies are able to raise two chicks to fledging; in poor years the smaller chick, from the second egg to hatch (the eggs usually hatch a day or two apart), will starve — its older, stronger sibling pushing it away from the feeding parent.

As the chicks grow they change color, becoming darker with a second coat of down. They also become more mobile and slightly more independent. Their flippers have almost grown to their full length but have yet to harden so they are long and floppy, almost dragging on the ground. When the chicks beg from their parents, their flippers wobble when they flap. Perhaps they're practicing swimming in the air. (The flippers will have hardened by the time the chicks are about six weeks old.)

Practicing swimming in the air

The chicks' heads are now tiny in comparison to their enormous bellies. They're a bit like fuzzy Buddhas.

Hunting

An unlucky chick

Beginning to display

Dismembering a chick

Threatening a skua

22 December

The day begins sunny, warm, lovely, but by evening it's windy and snowing.

A South Polar skua (a large bird similar to a gull) is hunting in the colony. It grabs an egg from an Adélie nest on the edge of one of the subcolonies. Immediately the penguins attack and fight off the skua. It drops the egg and stands a short distance away, waiting. At first the penguins are very wary. They charge the skua, and it backs off. Slowly the penguins calm down, become a little distracted. Watching carefully the skua notices the lack of concentration and in a flash it has the egg once more in its bill. A general clamor erupts, flapping of wings and flippers, alarm calls of penguins, and the skua flies off, the egg in its bill. Landing a short distance away the skua proceeds to peck through the thick, hard shell and slurp out the contents in long stringy globs. There are constant attempts by the skuas to steal eggs or chicks and I hear the squawks and peeps of the penguins throughout the day.

25 December: Christmas

The past two days have been unbelievably blustery—first clouds, then sunshine, then horizontal snow and wind, wind, wind. The noise of the rattling and shaking of our tents makes sleep difficult and the constant wind is tiresome.

Our Christmas tree is primitive. It is made out of an old piece of plastic fencing curled into a column and decorated with some old ornaments left by previous researchers, painted penguin cutouts, and origami birds.

I get a Christmas present while sitting on the telemetry hill: three Snow Petrels fly by, tracing the cliff edge in graceful arcs, brilliant white against the dark rocks and water. Lovely spirits of the Antarctic.

Our Christmas tree

My Christmas present — three Snow Petrels

Our telemetry sessions are getting longer. We are finding the Royds Adélies feeding to the north and to the west into McMurdo Sound. These foraging trips can take several days with the birds traveling up to 25 miles (40 kilometers). Once in the water Adélies can move quickly, porpoising and "flying" under the water. Their bodies are perfectly designed torpedoes covered with a dense waterproof mat of feathers and a thick layer of fat to keep them warm. They normally swim at 5 miles per hour (8 kilometers per hour) and can dive for up to six minutes to depths of 520 feet (170 meters). If pursued, they can swim up to 9 miles per hour (16 kilometers per hour), probably faster, for short distances.

We catch penguins for diet sampling when they come back from feeding. The breeders bringing back food for their chicks have distinctly large, full bellies.

This is our first day of weekly diet sampling. We do this to compare what the Adélies are eating at the three colonies. This is our most unpleasant task: we catch a penguin, fill it up with water, and make it vomit. Fortunately, we only need a sample large enough to identify what they are eating, so when they are released they still have food for their chicks. One sample collected was entirely Antarctic silverfish, *Pleurogramma antarcticum* — a thin fish, about 8 inches (20 centimeters) long, with enormous eyes. The rest of the samples were krill, *Euphausia crystallorophius*, a relative of the shrimp, about 1.25 inches (2.5 centimeters) long. There are hundreds of krill in the samples. It's hard to believe that the penguins catch these individually, one at a time, but they do. The most digested samples are very smelly.

PLEUROGRAMMA ANTARCTICUM, EUPHAUSIA CRYSTALLOROPHIUS (not to scale), and a sample jar full of krill

27 December

The birds are increasingly aggressive, frequently charging us as we move through the colony, trying to peck or flipper-slap us with their hard, paddle-like wings. Sometimes they just run up to us, raise their neck ruffs, and growl — a throaty noise that leaves nothing misunderstood: "GET OUT!" Not only the breeders behave this way but also the nonbreeders. All the penguins are excited by the activity of rearing chicks.

29 December

At this point in the season there are hundreds of nonbreeders visiting the colony, wandering in the hills around the camp and Shackleton's hut. I walk about the colony looking for returning birds banded as chicks at Cape Royds (and other colonies) in previous years. I find one digging a scrape and displaying by its natal subcolony (the subcolony where it hatched). This bird is a three-year-old, banded at Cape Royds. We know this by looking up the number on its band in a data file. It may return next year and attempt to breed as a four-year-old. It's practicing for the future, acquiring the skills that it will need for successful pairing and nest site selection.

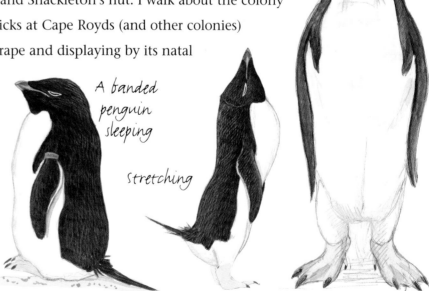

"GET OUT!"

A banded penguin sleeping

stretching

After finding this banded bird I continue through the colony. Strewn about on the ground are hundreds of penguin mummies, each in a contorted position. They vary in size from small chicks to large juveniles. As well as the intact mummies there are penguin bones, dried feet, flippers, and skulls picked clean by the skuas. These carcasses and penguin parts could be from last year or a few hundred years ago. The Antarctic is so dry and cold that nothing on land decomposes; it simply mummifies. I bend down and look closely at some bones a rather odd penguin has gathered to surround its nest with instead of rocks (we fondly call it the voodoo penguin). They are penguin bones: solid, thick, and flat — unlike the bones of flying birds, which are light, brittle, and hollow. The penguin bones act as ballast, like a scuba diver's weight belt, and the heavy-boned flippers make perfect oars for flying through the water (and slapping unwelcome biologists). These are adaptations to a life in the ocean, not a life in the air. It's eerie, the contrast between the life in the colony surrounding me, the displaying penguins, the begging chicks, and these mummies and bones.

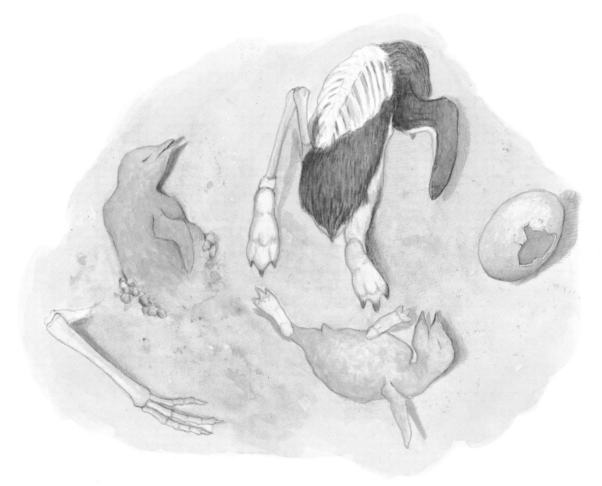

Penguin parts. Mummies of a small chick and an almost fully feathered chick; leg and foot bones and a broken penguin egg

An Adélie, clean from swimming, returns from foraging at sea to relieve its mate at the nest. The returning bird will open its beak to the begging chicks and regurgitate small amounts of krill into their waiting mouths. Some krill will dribble onto its chest—staining it like its mate's. The colony is now covered with maroon-colored guano (penguin poop).

The view south to Cape Barne with fast ice and distant Weddell seals

31 December

Our views can alter daily as the pack ice and the occasional convoy of icebergs, driven by the wind and currents, move in and out of McMurdo Sound. Today, due to a strong wind, thirty-five knots, from the southeast, all the fast ice has broken away from the land. Huge sheets of fast ice, a couple miles (several kilometers) long, move north to the Ross Sea. The wind and waves will break up the sheet to form floes, which may collect together and form pack ice. In a couple of hours our views have completely changed.

The view south to Cape Barne after the ice has broken out. A south Polar skua flies in the foreground.

01 January

We had a small gathering in our tent last night with some New Zealand guests from Scott Base to greet the New Year. Today is a normal day, with our usual tasks, although I do take a thorough sponge bath and wash my hair for the first time since we came out into the field. It feels great and I no longer smell like a penguin colony.

Cooling off

03 January

It's hot today, 34°F (1°C). The fuzzy chicks are sprawled on the ground panting with their feet stuck out behind to cool off. The adults do this too on particularly hot days. Penguin feet are fleshy and strong with long nails for digging scrapes in the hard ground and for traction on ice and snow. Underneath they have soft pads almost like a dog's and they flare out at the sides like the toes of a gecko. On top they are wrinkled and covered with fine scales. In color they range from purplish pink to pale pink, with nails from blackish to reddish-brown. They look painted. I love to look at penguin feet.

Penguin feet

05 January

Today the chicks seem suddenly larger, and more upright, sitting about with bellies extended, enormous feet thrust out. They are more mobile and begin to form groups of three or more, called crèches. These groupings are for protection from the skuas when both parents must leave to forage. As the chicks grow, they need more food. Now when the adults return from these trips they are chased about by peeping, rubbery-winged, demanding chicks that are rapidly increasing in size. Soon, at least in mass, the chicks will rival the size of the adults.

A crèche

08 January

We can see Weddell seals and penguins loafing everywhere on the remaining fast ice around Cape Royds. The Weddell seals, unlike the Adélie Penguins, spend their winter (March through September) in the far South. They will keep holes open in the solid sheet of fast ice that will cover McMurdo Sound when the temperature drops. They use these holes to breathe through when they are under the ice and as passages in and out of the water. As I watch them sleeping I hear a variety of weird grunting, snoring, popping, and whistling noises coming from under the ice: Weddell seals calling and singing.

Weddell seals are very fat with tiny heads, like inflated harbor seals. They are solely fish eaters — unlike another Antarctic species, the leopard seal, which eats penguins as well as krill.

A Weddell seal sleeping in the sun

12 January

Two leopard seals show up today. Their large mouths and their long, thin bodies give them a reptilian and predatory appearance. The Adélies, a major item in the leopard seal diet, are afraid to enter the water. Near the entrance of the colony one of the seals hunts. Conspicuous at times, it shows itself along the edge of a small ice floe or along the beachfront. Sometimes it disappears for a period, then suddenly reappears in the same area or a short distance away. It yawns, its mouth filled with curved and notched teeth. Several times it lunges upward out of the water at some penguins on a small floe.

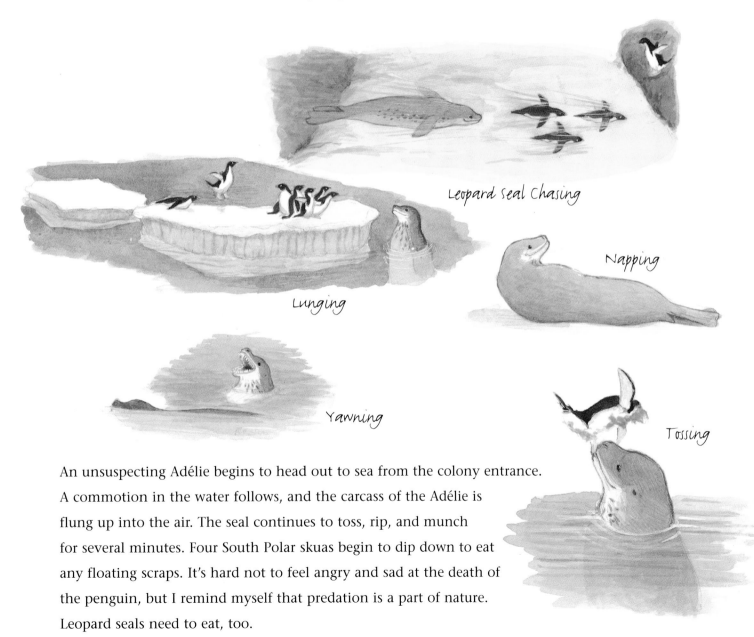

Leopard seal Chasing

Lunging

Napping

Yawning

Tossing

An unsuspecting Adélie begins to head out to sea from the colony entrance. A commotion in the water follows, and the carcass of the Adélie is flung up into the air. The seal continues to toss, rip, and munch for several minutes. Four South Polar skuas begin to dip down to eat any floating scraps. It's hard not to feel angry and sad at the death of the penguin, but I remind myself that predation is a part of nature. Leopard seals need to eat, too.

15 January

Cold day (22°F, −5°C). Wind from the northwest, then moving about in all directions.

Some of the adult female Adélies are looking tiny, and although the chicks are not as tall as these females they are often much rounder. The chicks are incredibly bottom-heavy with enormous rears. Their flippers are beginning to harden, their voices are changing. There is a lot of screeching, biting, and attempted slapping with semihardened flippers. It's difficult to believe that they will ever have the muscles to swim.

19 January

The breeding season is beginning to end. We count fewer breeders remaining in the colony. In the weigh-bridge plot I often can't find banded adults to go with known chicks at nest sites. This is because both members of the pair are often out foraging now that chicks are large enough to crèche and protect themselves from the skuas.

Most of the day today was spent counting the chicks in the colony: 4,609. With a total of 3,600 nests, average productivity per nest is 1.28 chicks, which means that over a quarter of the pairs successfully raised two chicks. A good year for the penguins.

The colony remains incredibly noisy and busy. Birds are displaying, copulating, and fighting. There are chicks running all over, chasing each other and any adult that's recently returned from foraging. Some chicks look moth-eaten, like pathetic, dirty, dandruffy gnomes; others have almost entirely lost their down and look like adults with white chins. I now hear very few soft, begging peeps coming out of the larger chicks, only odd squawks. They are beginning to mimic adult behavior with stretches, eye rolls, and ecstatic displays. They look ridiculous.

Birds continue to fight for territories and copulate.

21 January

It's funny watching chicks chase the adults when they return from the sea. After greeting its own chick the adult runs away, with an occasional glance over the shoulder, the screaming chick in pursuit. Suddenly the adult stops and turns around, wearing a somewhat frantic expression, eyes bugging out. The chick's open mouth disappears into the adult's mouth, the adult's neck stretches upward, some gulping motions follow, and the krill or fish is regurgitated into the waiting chick.

In the afternoon Sue and I weigh fifty chicks and measure their flippers to see how fast they are growing. We compare these weekly measurements with those taken at the other colonies to see if there are differences in growth rates. Despite their short legs and huge bodies, the chicks are quite swift and often difficult to catch. Once the chick is grabbed it's put into a bag and weighed, and its flipper is measured. One chick weighs 4.85 kilos (over 10 pounds)! It is enormous but still quite fuzzy. The chick is then released to return to either a crèche or its nest. By the end of the session we are covered with bits of chick down and poop.

Weighing a chick

23 January

An exquisite day, clear, calm, balmy, about 32°F (0°C) and with *no* wind; the first in ten days.

Ian and Sacha arrive from Cape Bird to help us break down camp and pack up. First we spend the morning banding chicks — our last major task to wrap up the season. By marking them we will know if they return to Cape Royds or wander to another colony in future years. We herd twenty to thirty chicks into a corral made of PVC piping and plastic netting. Once the chicks are penned, we hop in and sit or kneel, catch a chick, and put a band around its now hardened flipper. Some chicks are still downy while others are in the process of molting. Down and feather sheaths fly about making us cough. The chicks themselves cough, squawk, and peep.

We band four hundred chicks in one morning.

After lunch I pack up camp while the others take down the weigh bridge and fencing. Finally by 01:00 (1 A.M.) everything is boxed and weighed once again for the helicopter.

It's hard to believe that we leave tomorrow. My season with the penguins has flown by.

I walk down to the colony to say my last farewells to Cape Royds. It is beautiful: a still, clear evening, with McMurdo Sound covered in pack ice.

Soon the penguins will be leaving Cape Royds too. In a week or two the young will abandon their subcolonies and gather at the colony entrance to make their first plunges into the water. I can imagine a great deal of pushing and shoving to get "someone else" to go in first. Once in the water there will be a bit of panic, spluttering, and then finally confidence as the penguins realize they are in their element and on their own. They will have to learn through trial and error how to feed themselves and escape from predators.

In February, as the Polar night begins to approach the Antarctic, the young will begin a long journey north, migrating, following the pack ice as the Southern Ocean begins to freeze. The adults will leave separately, after spending two weeks molting on the pack ice or occasionally on land. At the outer portion of the pack ice zone (which lies 1,000 miles north of Cape Royds in the winter), all the penguins will spend the southern winter. As spring approaches in September, the adults will begin to feed frantically, fattening, before migrating to breed at Cape Royds. In November, when the adults return, the cycle will be completed.

The Adélie Penguins swimming north

The young of this year will spend the next two years in the pack ice. Only a few venture to land for several days next summer. When they are two or three years old they will return to the colony to practice nest building and perhaps to find a future mate.

A young Adélie showing the white chin that will become black like the adult's after its first molt next summer

I, too, will be heading north, back to California. Although it will be midwinter there, it will be warm in comparison to the Antarctic summer. There will be flush toilets, a comfortable bed, no layers of clothing and heavy parkas to wear, and darkness at night. But I will miss the penguins. I will miss the intensity of life in the colony: the antics of the begging chicks and the adults' fierce fights and odd displays (and their fleshy feet). And I will miss the beauty of Cape Royds and the simplicity of life in our small camp. Already I am hoping that I will be able to return next year to watch another season unfold in the Adélie Penguin colony.